Today I Write a Letter

Written by **Kimberly R. Abel**

Illustrated by **Margaret Willis**

Today I write a letter
To a boy so far away.
My teacher gave his name to me;
I don't know what to say
To one who speaks so strangely,
With a different color skin.
Living in a distant country,
What could I say to him?

3

I tap my pencil softly,

Thinking how I'd rather be

Riding downhill on my bike

Or swinging from a tree.

Or maybe I'd go fishing

In my grandpa's fishing hole

With some hooks, a can of worms,

My best friend, and a pole.

Do you think this boy who lives

So very far away

Plays any of the kinds of games

That I so like to play?

Do you think he likes to whistle
Or build castles in the sand,
Or swing on swings, or kick a ball,
Or watch a butterfly land?

I wonder . . .

Dear Masashi,

My name is Dave. I am eight years old. I like to fish and ride my bike and eat ice cream. What do you do in your country? Do you like to play games?

Yours truly,

Dave

Today I got a letter

From a boy not far away.

Listen while I read it.

Hear what he has to say.

Dear Dave,

Konnichiwa, good day! I am eight years old.

I like to go fishing in the ocean with my best friend, Hiro.

I like to ride bikes and play baseball. My favorite ice cream

is chocolate. Do you like to eat rice?

Mata,

Masashi

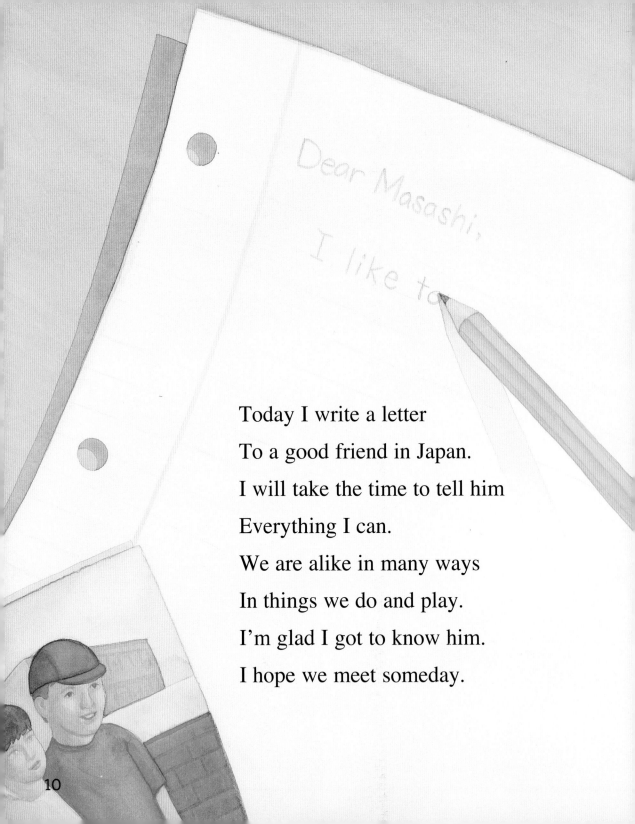

Dear Masashi,

I like to

Today I write a letter
To a good friend in Japan.
I will take the time to tell him
Everything I can.
We are alike in many ways
In things we do and play.
I'm glad I got to know him.
I hope we meet someday.